PUSS IN BOOTS

Paul Galdone

SCHOLASTIC INC.
New York Toronto London Auckland Sydney Tokyo

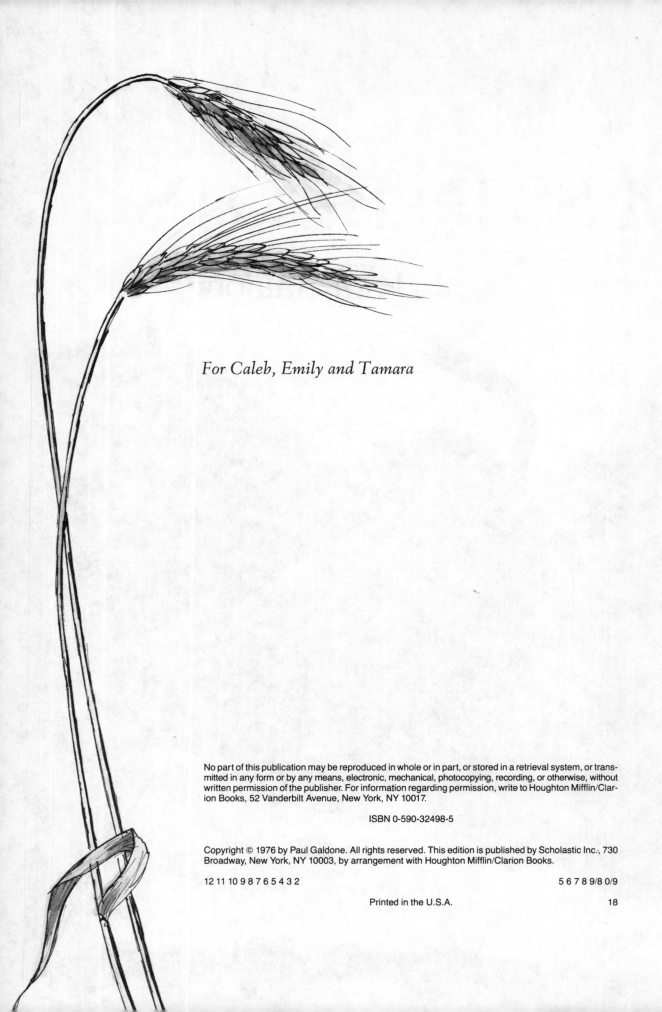

For Caleb, Emily and Tamara

ISBN 0-590-32498-5

12 11 10 9 8 7 6 5 4 3 2   5 6 7 8 9/8 0/9

Printed in the U.S.A.

Once long ago there was a miller. When he became so old that he could no longer work, he divided his property among his three sons.

He left the mill to his oldest son,

and the donkey to his second son.

To his youngest son he left the cat, Puss.

The youngest son was very sad.

"My brothers can use the mill and the donkey to work together," he said. "But how can I ever make a living with just this cat?"

Now Puss was a clever cat and could understand what people said.

"Cheer up!" Puss said to the youngest son. "Have a pair of boots made for me so that I can run through the sharp brambles, and get me a sack with a cord. If you do this, you will never be unhappy again."

The miller's son was very surprised to hear the cat speak, but he did as Puss told him. He got Puss a sack with a strong cord and he had a fine pair of red leather boots made to the cat's size.

When Puss had learned to run in his new boots, he went to the bramble patch where many wild rabbits lived. Puss put some cabbage leaves and parsley and two carrots in the sack. Then he hid behind a tree and waited.

Soon a foolish young rabbit came along and hopped right into the sack. Puss quickly pulled tight the cord. He slung the sack over his shoulder and hurried to the King's castle.

Puss knocked at the door. Out came the King and his guards.

"How do you do, your Majesty," said Puss. "My master, the Marquis of Carabas, sends this rabbit to you."

"I have never heard of the Marquis of Carabas," exclaimed the King. "But I am very fond of fresh game, so I shall gladly accept this present."

The next day Puss went off to a wheat field. He filled the sack with golden grain. Then he hid in the high grass and made the sound of a partridge. Soon a pair of foolish partridges heard the call and ran into the sack.

Puss pulled tight the cord on the sack and hurried to the King's castle.

"Good day, your Majesty," said Puss. "The Marquis of Carabas hopes that you will enjoy these birds at your dinner table."

"They are indeed fine birds," replied the King. He smacked his lips and called to his guards, "See that Cook prepares these at once!"

On the third morning Puss caught two large trout and brought them to the King, too.

"Here is another gift from my lord, the Marquis of Carabas," explained Puss. The King was very pleased.

He patted his round belly and said, "The Marquis must be a fine person to send me all these tasty treats."

As Puss was leaving, he heard the King's coachmen talking.

"The King has ordered that we ready his coach for a ride along the river today," said one.

"And he will be taking his daughter, the princess, with him," replied the other.

Puss ran all the way from the King's castle to the youngest son's house.

"Master," he cried, "today your fortune will be made! All you must do is go for a swim in the river. Leave the rest to me."

The miller's son did as Puss told him. He went to the river, took off his clothes, and jumped into the water. While he practiced floating, Puss hid the young man's ragged clothes behind a rock.

No sooner had Puss done this than the King's coach drove up.
"Help, Help!" Puss yelled as he ran into the road. "The
Marquis of Carabas has been robbed!"

When the King heard this,
he stuck his head out of the window.

"Stop the coach," he ordered. He recognized Puss and he remembered the many tasty gifts Puss's master had given to him.

"Your Majesty, someone has stolen my master's clothes," said Puss.

"Footman," the King ordered, "run back to the castle and fetch one of my best suits for the Marquis of Carabas."

The miller's son was very surprised.

"Who is the Marquis of Carabas?" he whispered to Puss.

"I have told the King that you are the Marquis," Puss whispered in reply.

The miller's son dressed in the rich suit of clothes and, indeed, he looked as splendid as any Marquis.

"Now you must thank the King," said Puss. "Leave the rest to me and your fortune will soon be made."

The miller's son thanked the King politely for the new clothes. "You are most welcome," replied the King. "Now would you please join us for a ride in the coach." The miller's son sat next to the Princess, who was happy to see such a handsome young man.

Puss ran ahead till he came to a field where some haymakers were working.

"Haymakers!" called Puss in a fierce voice. "When the King drives past and asks to whom this field belongs, you must reply, 'To the Marquis of Carabas.' If you don't, I shall chop you fine as mincemeat."

Soon the King passed by in his coach.

"To whom does this fine hayfield belong?" he asked.

"To our lord, the Marquis of Carabas," replied the haymakers, for they had been greatly frightened by Puss.

Then Puss ran on till he came to a field where some reapers were working.

"Reapers!" called Puss in an even fiercer voice than before. "When the King drives past and asks to whom this field belongs, you must reply, 'To the Marquis of Carabas.' If you don't, I shall chop you fine as mincemeat!"

Soon the King passed by in his coach.

"To whom does this fine field of grain belong?" he asked.

"To our lord, the Marquis of Carabas," replied the reapers, for they too had been greatly frightened by Puss.

"You have very fine land," the King said to the miller's son.

The young man saw what Puss was up to and said nothing. But he smiled at the Princess and she smiled back at him.

Puss ran as hard as his boots could carry him till he came to a great castle.

The castle belonged to a wicked old Giant. The Giant owned all the lands the King had just passed by, and for years he had forced the haymakers and reapers to work for him.

Puss had heard that the Giant also possessed the powers of a magician.

"What do you want?" the Giant roared when he saw it was only a cat who had disturbed him.

"I could not pass this way," Puss replied, "without paying respect to the most famous of magicians."

This greatly pleased the Giant, who let Puss into his hall.

"Is it really true that you can change yourself into a lion or an elephant or anything you choose?" asked Puss.

"Oh, yes, I can change into many animals," grinned the Giant.

BOOM! A loud clap of thunder echoed through the castle and there stood an elephant.

"Amazing!" exclaimed Puss, who stood out of the way of the swinging trunk.

Suddenly the elephant roared and there stood a lion.

"How fantastic!" cried Puss, though he was very much afraid. "It must be easy for you to turn into something large. But can you also turn into something small?"

"Yes!" roared the lion, and in an instant a little mouse scurried across the floor.

That was just what Puss had been waiting for.

With one pounce he caught the mouse and ate it up.

And that was the end of the wicked old Giant.

By and by the King's coach arrived at the Giant's castle.

"Welcome to the castle of the Marquis of Carabas," Puss announced with a bow.

"Does this beautiful castle belong to you, too, my lord Marquis?" asked the King. He was greatly impressed.

Puss brought them all to the dining hall.

There a great feast had been prepared by the servants, who were much happier obeying Puss than the wicked Giant.

The King was very pleased with the handsome young Marquis and his castle and all his lands. "You may ask my daughter to marry you, since you both seem so fond of each other."

The Princess agreed, and they had the wedding that very afternoon.

There was a great celebration
that lasted long into the night.
Puss in his red leather boots led all the dances.

"Thank you for all your help," the miller's son told Puss, when the merriment was finally over.

Next day he had a special throne made for Puss. And they all lived happily ever after.